library 2000
GREAT INVENTIONS
DISCOVERIES AND INVENTIONS
FAMOUS ARTISTS AND COMPOSERS
SHIPS

Published in Great Britain by Frederick Warne (Publishers) Ltd, London, 1979
Copyright © AFHA Internacional S.A., Barcelona, Spain, 1972
English translation copyright © Frederick Warne (Publishers) Ltd, 1979

ISBN 0 7232 2340 8

Phototypeset by Tradespools Ltd, Frome, Somerset

Printed in Spain by Emograph S.A., Barcelona

library 2000

Illustrated by Vincent Segrelles

Written by Antonio Cunillera

Translated by Caroline Hillier

Great Inventions

FREDERICK WARNE

CONTENTS

INTRODUCTION

This book introduces the reader to the most important of man's inventions, which have opened the way to technical progress at all levels. The inventions chosen are those which are considered revolutionary, those which have marked a decisive step forward for mankind and which have had countless applications in daily life and in the realms of industry, science and art.

These great discoveries, often made as a result of immense effort, despite difficulties and failure, by men who were not understood by their contemporaries, often had unexpected and far-reaching results. The men who invented the wheel, the raft and the magic lantern, for instance, were not able to appreciate fully the importance of their inventions at the time. Designed to fulfil specific purposes, these devices incorporate concepts which have proved capable of almost infinite development. Modern technology depends upon these concepts, and without the initial inventions such technology would not have evolved. The inventor is one of the principle architects of civilization.

THE WHEEL

No one knows who first invented the wheel. As with other inventions in the distant past, it was probably the work of several generations.

In ancient times, men knew how to use stone weapons, the bow, metals, rafts, the lathe, the loom, the drill, the sledge and the plough before they invented the wheel. Before this, men carried everything on their backs, or on the backs of animals. It is possible that the primitive rollers used for putting under a load inspired the earliest use of the wheel. The first proper wheels we know about in history however were those used in Ur, in about 2500 BC. At first the wheel was made of solid wood, and was very large and clumsy. To make it faster and more easy to manoeuvre, sections were cut out, forming a spoked wheel.

Shown below are four types of wheel: the wheel from Mercurago in Italy of about 1000 BC, an Egyptian wheel of the sixteenth century BC, an Etruscan wheel of about 400 BC, and a Roman wheel of 100 BC. The wheel was applied to locomotion and the chariot was invented before horses were in use as domestic animals; the earliest chariots were probably hauled by oxen. The illustration shows a Sumerian chariot, one of the first to be built, with four solid wheels and a raised guard.

Did you know . . .

. . . that there is a legend which tells how the wheel was invented by a Chinese philosopher who spent day after day watching the circular movement of a flower's corolla blown by the wind?

. . . that the earliest wheels were wooden, but were not in fact made from one piece of wood? As it was difficult to find pieces of wood which were large enough, craftsmen made up the circular shape from three segments. They nailed them together and because the wood wore out, they protected it with rudimentary tyres, or bands of leather finished with copper studs.

Mercurago wheel   *Egyptian wheel*   *Etruscan wheel*   *Roman wheel*

In the illustration on the left, wooden rollers are being used to move a large block of stone. The rollers were placed underneath the stone and the block was pushed by slaves, straining as hard as they could. It slid gradually forwards until it reached the right place. The wheel and the cart meant that less time and effort were needed. In the right-hand illustration is a medieval cart with bell-shaped wheels and a shaft to which the horse could be harnessed.

The wheel was an invention which had many uses, including the water-wheel. The water may drive the wheel round as a source of power, or the bucket-like sections which dip into the water may be used to carry it up to irrigate the ground.

After the Middle Ages, when chariots were no longer used, more comfortable means of transport began to be developed. People travelled in large closed-in passenger coaches drawn by up to six horses.

Cog-wheels, which employ interlocking teeth to transmit a rotary movement between two axles, are used in many machines and motors. The wheel in all its forms is still a basic element of most mechanical devices.

A tyre is a rubber tube, filled with compressed air and protected by a strong outer covering also made of rubber. When fitted to the wheel it helps absorb shock and improves roadholding.

GUNPOWDER

In the Middle Ages, the outcome of battles in Europe depended mainly on knights, who were trained in single combat from a very early age. They would fight armed with a lance and sword protected from head to foot in heavy armour. But one day in 1300 an incredible event occurred which was in time to change the history of the whole world. A German monk and alchemist called Berthold Schwartz, or Berthold the Black, discovered by chance the formula for making gunpowder. Some say the formula had already been discovered over a hundred years earlier by the English monk Roger Bacon; it was certainly known in China and Arabia. The introduction of firearms, using gunpowder, made armour virtually useless and put an end to the Age of Chivalry. Some people consider that gunpowder made all fighting men equal, and helped bring about the death of feudalism.

A series of weapons, making use of the new discovery, were invented; the cannon was one of them. One of the most famous surviving cannons is Mons Meg, now at Edinburgh Castle. It was built by the smith Moses McKim, in the mid-fifteenth century. It is 5m long, with a calibre of 50cm.

Helm with vizor

The cannon Mons Meg

A blunderbuss

A Colt revolver

Berthold the Black mixed sulphur and saltpetre and added vegetable charcoal. An explosion nearly cost him his life and orange flames shot from the black powder; he had discovered gunpowder.

The Chinese invented gunpowder much earlier than the Europeans, because by the eleventh century they were already experts at making fireworks and at firing rockets.

Medieval armour, before the invention of gunpowder.

Military dress of a soldier with gun and sword.

Because the advent of firearms made armour ineffective, gunpowder had a great influence on fighting dress. The introduction of cannons also led to new methods of warfare being evolved. Fortifications could be defended by a few men on the battlements of a castle.

New tactics were gradually introduced. Castles were no longer necessary for defence, and no longer had to be stormed. Artillery meant that fortifications like those in the picture could be used. There was no need to go into a town to capture it. Cannon-fire could cause terrible losses among the besieged from a distance. Note the system of trenches, the ammunition store and the gun emplacements.

Guns were later used at sea. Instead of boarding ships in a battle, well-placed cannon could cause terrible damage and even sink ships. After gunpowder came dynamite, invented by Nobel in 1871. This and other more powerful explosives enabled bigger and more effective weapons to be developed. In the next century, iron-clad battleships with a gun range of several miles were to rule the sea.

Lead bullet at the top; powder in the middle; and primer at the bottom.

PRINTING

A piece of metal moveable type, shaped in a bronze matrix, used in printing.

Did you know . . .

. . . that the oldest book in the world was printed in China, using hand-cut wood blocks?

. . . that although it was time-consuming to write books by hand, there were proper libraries in ancient times?

. . . that the Gutenberg Bible was the first printed book in Europe, made in the fifteenth century by a German called Gutenberg?

For centuries, men wrote on stone, on parchment or papyrus. Before the invention of the alphabet, they represented ideas by means of picture signs, called hieroglyphs. Once the alphabet had been invented, everything was handwritten, but this was very tiring and had to be carried out by numerous scribes.

The first printing presses were made of wood. The press illustrated above is of the time of Johann Gutenberg, who had set up a primitive block-printing press in about 1430. While he was busy cutting precious stones and making mirrors, Gutenberg was also working on a secret technique for making a printing press with metal moveable type. Such a press was built in 1450. Metal type was set into a matrix on a metal sheet, letter by letter, to make the appropriate words, and then inked. Another sheet of metal was screwed down to press a sheet of paper against the type. Thanks to this invention, knowledge eventually ceased to be the privilege of the few.

Stone tablet with Egyptian hieroglyphs.

Page of a book written and decorated by hand in the Middle Ages.

The first book printed on Gutenberg's press was the Bible. All the books printed between 1455 and 1530 are called 'incunabula'. There are about 450.000 of them.

In 1440, Gutenberg pretended to be busy working on precious stones and making mirrors, so that he was able to keep his research a secret. The new invention opened up new horizons for mankind.

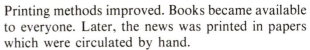

A view of a printing workshop: two compositors in the background are setting type and inking it. In the foreground a proof-reader is correcting proofs.

Printing methods improved. Books became available to everyone. Later, the news was printed in papers which were circulated by hand.

Books and newspapers are printed more and more quickly. A Linotype machine sets whole lines of type in one piece. It is a composing machine with matrices.

Printing techniques have been perfected in accordance with today's technological expertise. Above is a machine similar to the one used to print this book.

LENSES

Not much was known about lenses in ancient times. Men knew how to make glass, but only used it to make little receptacles and ornaments. Only a few people were interested in the optical properties of glass. The practice of placing a lens in front of the eye was generally adopted for the first time in the thirteenth century. We don't know much about the inventor or the date and place of his discovery. Some people think it must have been the work of an illiterate craftsman, probably a glazier, who made ornaments and panes of glass for windows. Other people attribute the discovery of lenses to the Dominican monk Allessandro della Spina in 1285.

The principle of lenses was probably discovered by observation. Drops of water form natural lenses. Look at one on a leaf and you will see that the surface of the leaf appears to be enlarged. When the technique of making lenses had been perfected, the idea of using two lenses to see distant objects was born. This was first done in Holland. Galileo heard of this invention and used the lenses to make an instrument which he called the telescope, for looking at the sky. It was perfected in 1680, when Newton invented the mirror telescope, seen in the picture below. The microscope was invented at the same time as the first optical lenses.

Did you know . . .

. . . that when the Emperor Nero watched displays in the amphitheatre, he held a precious stone with curved facets, which were probably concave, in front of one of his eyes to correct his short-sightedness?

. . . that Archimedes had studied the way concave mirrors can concentrate rays of light on a particular spot and is said to have used the idea to build mirrors which would set fire, from a distance, to the Roman ships which were attacking his town?

Spectacles with lenses close together were used in the Middle Ages. People thought they should be in the middle of the face and not directly in front of the eyes.

Lenses enabled men to see farther. As soon as the first spectacles were made, there was a demand for highly polished glass, which was supplied by skilled polishers.

Spectacles we use today have frames made from tortoiseshell or plastic and are moulded to fit the facial contours.

A Dutchman called Lippershey, a spectacle-maker in Middelburg, had made a telescope before Galileo, using lenses in a tube. In 1608, he applied to the Dutch government for a patent for his invention for 30 years. Others think that the discovery was made by Zacharias Janssen, who built a telescope in 1608, or by Jacob Adrinsson, also known as Matius.

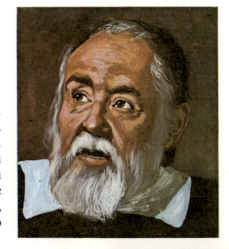

Galileo, the inventor of the first refracting telescope

In the second half of the eighteenth century, in about 1789, the German astronomer Herschel built a telescope like the one shown on the right. It was 1.5m in diameter and over 13m high. In the illustration on the far right you can see the telescope on the Mount Wilson Observatory in California. The mirror has a diameter of 2.5m.

We owe the first really good microscope to the Dutchman van Leeuwenhoek. The first illustration on the left shows Galileo's microscope. The second illustration is a microscope made in London by Harris & Son in the eighteenth century. Over the years better and better microscopes were made, and today we have the electron microscope, which enables us to get amazing results in the fields of science and industry. On the right you can see what an atom looks like.

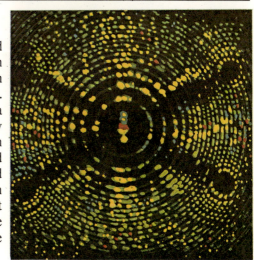

THE PLOUGH

From very early times the human race has tried to cultivate the land. Men soon realized however that they must till the soil to prevent it from becoming impoverished. In order to do this they developed the first ploughs. These turned over the soil and, when combined with a primitive form of crop rotation, allowed the same fields to be used year after year. Permanent villages grew up around the fields, with a settled way of life based on agriculture. The development of large towns was only possible because they could be supplied with quantities of grain, cereals, vegetables, fruit and other produce—the surplus produced by the agricultural communities. In the illustration you can see a type of multiple plough with seven ploughshares, made in the United States and used for ploughing over vast tracts of land.

Hoe   *Sickle*   *Shovel*

16

*Primitive plough
of bronze and wood*

The first plough was a clumsy pick, like a rough branch, pushed and pulled by several men to enable them to turn over the clods of earth. Later, oxen replaced men.

Men discovered bronze, which could be used in many ways. Ploughs were made of wood and bronze, and man now had a much stronger agricultural tool. In the illustration above, the different parts of such a plough can be seen.

Because it was so important to the economy, many further changes were made in the way the plough was constructed. The ploughshare and wheel were added (left), making it more efficient.

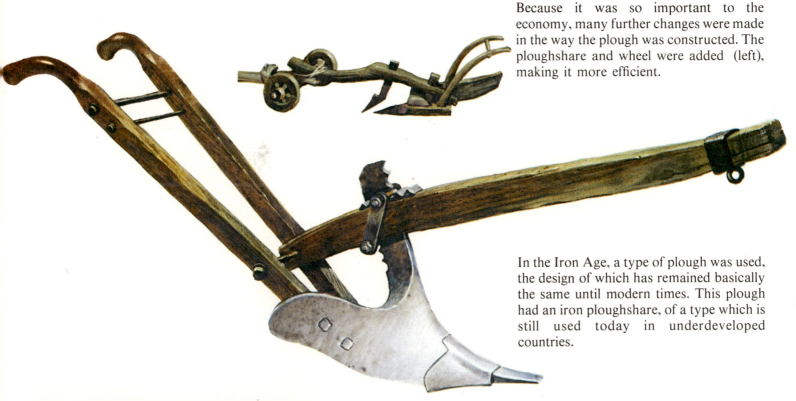

In the Iron Age, a type of plough was used, the design of which has remained basically the same until modern times. This plough had an iron ploughshare, of a type which is still used today in underdeveloped countries.

The primitive plough which our ancestors used to cultivate the soil has evolved into a modern machine, which can be driven almost effortlessly. On the left, a modern agricultural tractor being used for ploughing.

Another machine which helps to make work on the land easier: the combine harvester which is now used all over the world.

THE LATHE

The lathe is one of man's most useful and practical inventions, and can be adapted in many ways. As a machine-tool it has enabled industry to develop to an extremely high level, but this invention, which has led in our day to highly efficient automated machines, was already known in ancient times. The first lathe was a simple tool, in which a small-diameter cylinder, the material to be shaped, was joined to a wheel or crank of large diameter. The axis rested on two supports. Power was generated by the wheel or crank, and a cutting tool held against the work to produce an evenly turned result.

The lathe is a machine which is used to round off pieces of wood, metal, and similar materials. A series of machines is derived from it: for example machines to mill, to straighten, to file and to pierce. Without the lathe we would be without cars, trains, ships, and many other everyday things. It is one of the basic tools used in the production of every kind of machine.

Lathe-turned railway axle

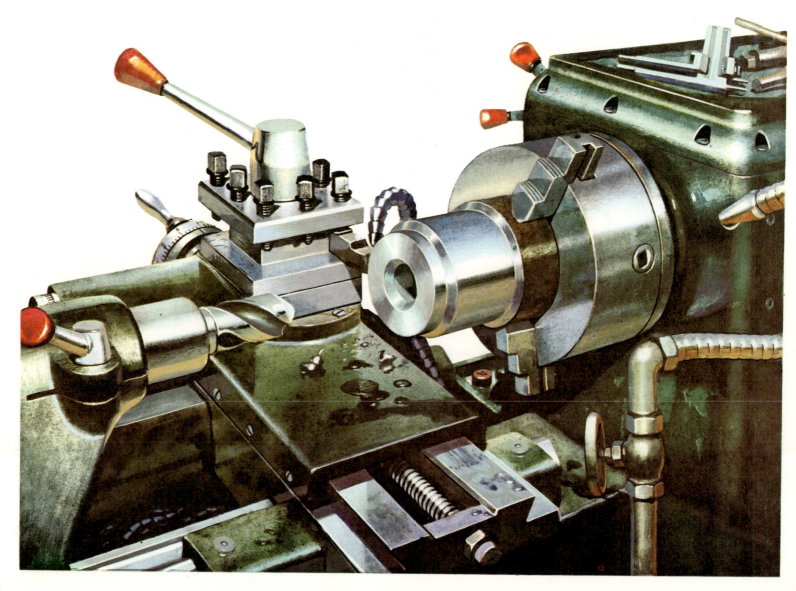

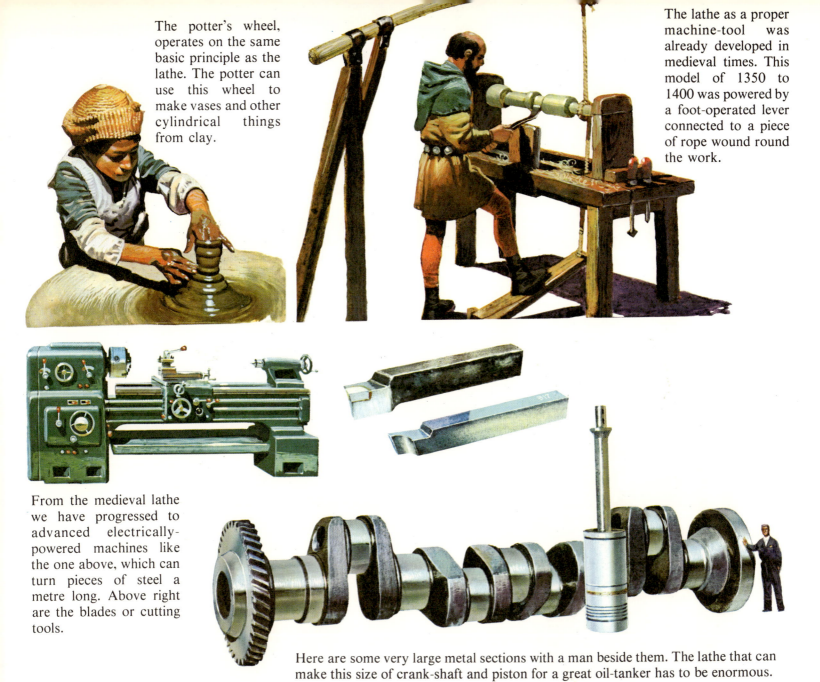

The potter's wheel, operates on the same basic principle as the lathe. The potter can use this wheel to make vases and other cylindrical things from clay.

The lathe as a proper machine-tool was already developed in medieval times. This model of 1350 to 1400 was powered by a foot-operated lever connected to a piece of rope wound round the work.

From the medieval lathe we have progressed to advanced electrically-powered machines like the one above, which can turn pieces of steel a metre long. Above right are the blades or cutting tools.

Here are some very large metal sections with a man beside them. The lathe that can make this size of crank-shaft and piston for a great oil-tanker has to be enormous.

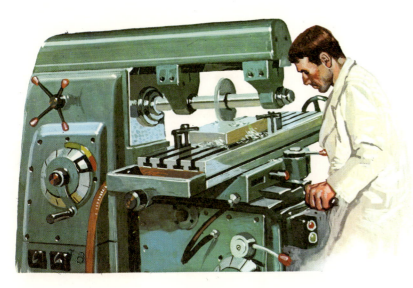

The lathe has become more and more technically perfect. Above you can see an example of a milling machine, which uses a moving rotating tool to make a flat cut. All the operator has to do is fix the part on it and set the tool in motion.

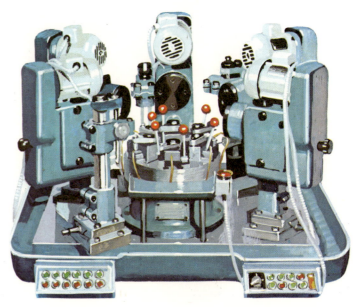

A 'transfer' machine is a combination machine-tool for making special types of parts, using a number of different processes. A vast number of parts can be made quickly.

THE CLOCK

The invention of the clock gratified man's desire to measure time, a concept prehistoric man could understand because of the rhythms of his life, the changing seasons, the growth of his children and the way his own body grew old.

Before developing the clocks we know today, people told the time in other ways. The oldest method was the shadow-clock. This was a stick standing upright in the ground; the shadow it cast moved round it according to the sun. Then came sundials like the one you can see in the illustration below. In ancient times clepsydras or water-clocks were used: in the water-clock illustrated below the water sinking in the container made the cherub on the left rise, marking the hours with his pointer. Another type of clock was the sand-glass. But all these became old fashioned when the first mechanical clock appeared, like the clock with weights which you can see in the large illustration. A system of weighted cords wound round the wheels gave the mechanism continuous movement, which was governed by the regular oscillation of a weighted beam. This was really the first mechanical clock.

Did you know...

... that when they tried to replace the bells of Christian churches, Arabs were the first to experiment with making mechanical clocks?

... that in Venice there is a famous clock called The Moors, which shows the phases of the moon and the movements of the sun, and that two Moors strike the hours with a hammer on a bronze bell?

... that it was Galileo who discovered the regular swing of a pendulum, by watching the movement of a great bronze lamp in the cathedral in Pisa? The swinging pendulum proved to be a far more accurate controlling device than the weighted beam, and was generally adopted in the seventeenth century.

A shadow-clock,
an ancient sundial

A clepsydra
or water-clock

An hour- or sand-glass

The balance wheel and hairspring, invented by the Dutchman Huygens in the seventeenth century. It replaced the pendulum.

The movement of a clock is governed by what is called the escapement. The mainspring turns a toothed wheel which pushes against the ends of the anchor. This is attached to the swinging pendulum or balance wheel. As the anchor rocks, the wheel is allowed to rotate one tooth at a time. The rotating toothed wheel drives the hands of the clock, and the pressure of the spring transmitted through the anchor keeps the pendulum swinging.

The clock became a sign of wealth, an important ornament in the houses of the aristocracy and middle classes. Here is an eighteenth-century table clock surmounted by a representation of a cherub.

A famous English clock is mounted in the tower of Big Ben. It is well known for its chimes.

An early watch called a 'small tambour', made in the seventeenth century. This era saw the first of the well-made and extremely decorative watches, but they were still not very accurate.

Left: In 1760 John Harrison invented the chronometer, designed for accurate time-keeping at sea. Once the high-precision mechanism had been developed, the watch industry as we know it came into being.

Right: A caesium clock, based on the oscillations of an electron of an atom of caesium. It is accurate to millionths of a second.

THE LOOM

People knew how to spin and weave in prehistoric times. They learnt how to get wool from animals and which vegetable fibres to use. They did this because they wanted to cover their bodies with something finer and more decorative than animal skins.

Although other more rudimentary methods had been tried, the primitive loom proved the most effective method of weaving. The mechanical loom shown above, made from wood, cords, metal parts and weights, came in the intermediate stage between primitive craftsmen and the modern textile industry. Without looms people would be unable to have the choice of clothes that they have today.

Did you know . . .

. . . that the technique of plaiting rushes or vegetable fibres came before the invention of weaving, and that there were hand-plaited mats five thousand years before Christ?

. . . that spinning was first thought of when rope was invented, because when they plaited strands of coconut fibre, flax or camelhair, people realized that the tighter the strands were twisted, the stronger the cord became?

Primitive man using a distaff.

A primitive loom of ancient times, worked mainly by hand. Weights kept the threads hanging tautly from the chain. The woman lifted them one by one with her left hand so that she could weave the 'weft' thread through. Also all the alternate threads could be lifted at once by using horizontal bars called 'heddles'. Fine material could be woven either way.

A shuttle

The machine invented by Cartwright in 1784, made with wooden bars, pulleys and cranks. The invention contributed to what is called the Industrial Revolution.

In 1773 John Kay invented the fly-shuttle which was no longer pushed through by hand but run through by a system of pulleys. The craft of weaving became an industry.

The new looms angered the hand-loom weavers, who lost their jobs because of them, and the workmen attacked Kay's house. He had to escape through a window.

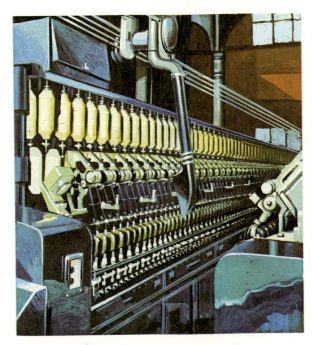

Left: Improvements to the loom, begun by Hargreaves, Arkwright, Kay and Crompton and continued by Cartwright and Jacquard, brought about a real industrial revolution.

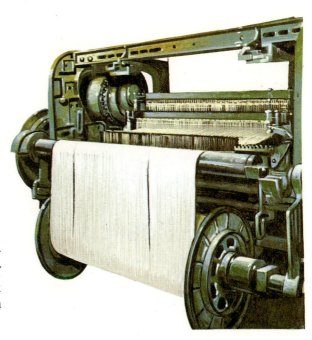

Right: Modern spinning and weaving machines with their hundreds of bobbins and kilometres of thread are an important part of our civilization today.

THE STEAMSHIP

The first sailor must have been a man clinging to a log. He must soon have realized that if he sat astride the log and pushed it along with a long branch that touched the bottom, he could choose the direction to go in and the rate of travel. The development of sails meant that the sailor no longer had to use his own strength to propel the boat; propulsion was provided by the wind. This meant however that he was at the mercy of the strength and direction of the wind, and sea voyages against the direction of the prevailing wind could take many months. The application of steam power to ships solved this problem, and allowed long voyages to be undertaken in a relatively short time which could be calculated in advance.

Did you know . . .

. . . that it was a Spaniard, Blasco de Garay, who first used a tank of boiling water aboard his ship the *Trinity*, to try to make it go by steam power?

. . . that a Frenchman, Denis Papin, finally succeeded in 1707 in adapting the steam engine that he had invented for use on a ship?

A raft

Egyptian boat

Galleon

The *Savannah, the first transatlantic steamship, 1819.*

24

In 1807 the American Fulton built a steamship in the United States, the *Clermont*, which was driven by paddlewheels. It crossed from New York to Albany.

In spite of Fulton's success, and although many other steamships were built, the sailing ships were slow to disappear.

In 1858, the *Great Eastern* was launched in London. She was the largest steamship of her day. She could carry 4,000 passengers at a maximum speed of 15 knots.

Riverboats, which employed a single stern paddlewheel, were very successful. The *Louisiana*, which plied up and down the Mississippi, saved people time and money.

The iron-clad ship appeared and in the late nineteenth century the steamship was adapted for war; it had guns and armoured swivel gun turrets with which to confront the enemy. Above is a Japanese warship of World War I.

Man's great conquests are rarely without their tragic side. The *Titanic*, the pride of the British line, the great transatlantic liner which was said to be unsinkable, struck an iceberg and sank on her maiden voyage in 1912.

THE BALLOON

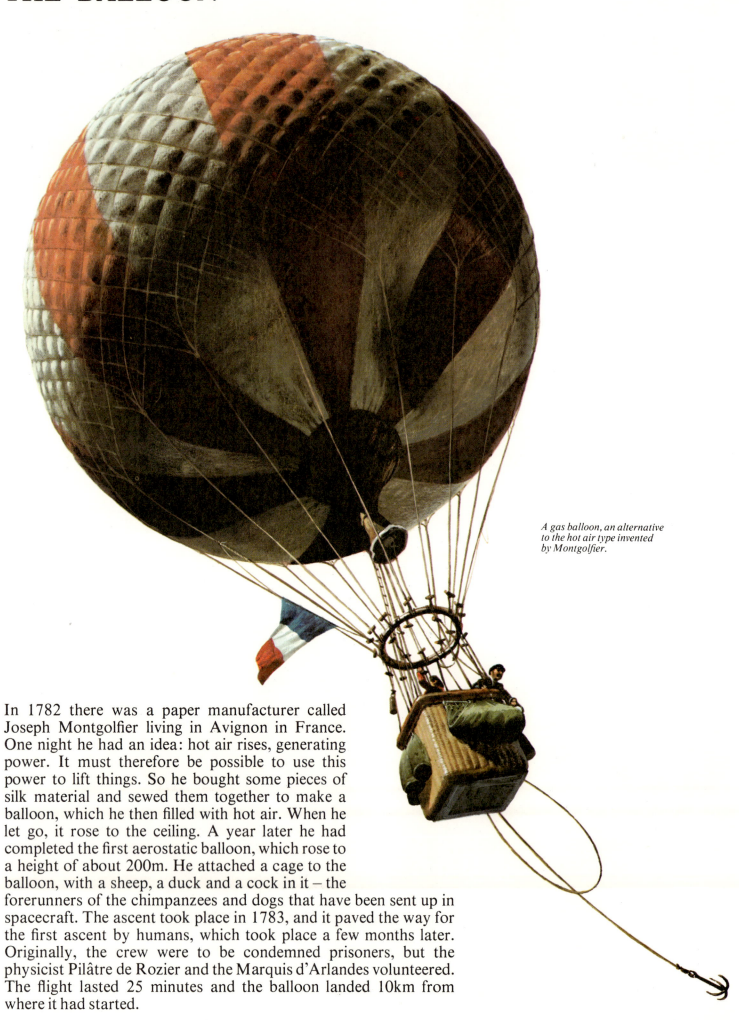

A gas balloon, an alternative to the hot air type invented by Montgolfier.

In 1782 there was a paper manufacturer called Joseph Montgolfier living in Avignon in France. One night he had an idea: hot air rises, generating power. It must therefore be possible to use this power to lift things. So he bought some pieces of silk material and sewed them together to make a balloon, which he then filled with hot air. When he let go, it rose to the ceiling. A year later he had completed the first aerostatic balloon, which rose to a height of about 200m. He attached a cage to the balloon, with a sheep, a duck and a cock in it – the forerunners of the chimpanzees and dogs that have been sent up in spacecraft. The ascent took place in 1783, and it paved the way for the first ascent by humans, which took place a few months later. Originally, the crew were to be condemned prisoners, but the physicist Pilâtre de Rozier and the Marquis d'Arlandes volunteered. The flight lasted 25 minutes and the balloon landed 10km from where it had started.

Before the Montgolfier balloons, a French Jesuit called De Lana had experimented unsuccessfully with an idea for an airship fitted with four metal spheres in which a vacuum had been created.

The first balloon built by the Frenchman Montgolfier: it made an ascent from Versailles, watched by a crowd of amazed spectators. It was man's first flight.

The greatest drawback of the balloon was that it was almost impossible to guide it. So the dirigible or navigable airship was developed, thanks to the work of Meusnier, Giffard and other inventors, including Count Zeppelin. The illustration shows Santos Dumont's dirigible, coming down in the garden of a house.

German airships designed by Zeppelin bombed London in World War I.

A Zeppelin in flames. The airship was slow, inadequately armed, and filled with highly dangerous inflammable gas, and it was soon superseded.

The dirigible was used in the conquest of the North Pole. The *Norge* airship is shown landing at Roy Bay, during its Polar expedition in 1926.

The nacelle or car of a balloon. It can be used by a lookout.

When the age of supersonic aircraft arrived, it looked as though dirigibles had had their day. But the construction of a new type of dirigible, the Aeron III (above), shows that the United States is still interested in this type of craft.

The conquest of the air has had its victims. The *Hindenburg* was destroyed by fire in five minutes in 1937, while landing at Lakehurst airport near New York.

Today sounding-balloons are used to study the upper layers of the atmosphere, and to enable astronomical observations to be made with ease.

THE RAILWAY

The railway was based on a very simple idea. Rails already existed and had been used since Henry IV's reign in the English mines; they had been invented by a man called Beaumont, who used them for coal wagons. The steam engine had also been used by Papin to propel a boat. What would happen if a steam engine was made to go along rails? Two men had the idea at the same time – Vivian and Trevithick. The latter was an English engineer who in 1800 built an engine which he succeeded in running along rails in Cornwall. He did it for a bet of 500 pounds. It wasn't very successful, but in time he perfected his engine and it became a fairground attraction. Eventually the invention ceased to be a fairground spectacle, challenged the horse-drawn vehicles and became the new mode of transport. This was largely due to George Stephenson, who in 1829 demonstrated a very efficient engine called the *Rocket* and proved the practicality of the railways.

Other engineers perfected bridging and tunnelling techniques, and railway systems were built all over the world.

The large steam engine in the picture above is of the 'Confederate' type, designed to pull long trains. Steam engines have now been almost entirely superseded by diesel and electric locomotives.

Did you know . . .

. . . that the first passenger train was driven by Stephenson himself, and that his engine drew six wagons loaded with iron and coal, and a number of carriages with 400 people on board?

. . . that it took a long time to persuade people to use the railways because they were frightened of the new invention and thought it might prove harmful?

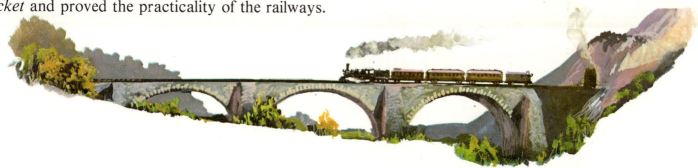

In 1829 there was a competition in England with a prize for the best engine. Stephenson's *Rocket* won the contest without difficulty. It weighed several tonnes and did 50km in two hours six minutes. A tremendous speed in those days!

An American train of the late nineteenth century. The guard iron in front of the engine was for clearing objects from the rails.

To encourage people to travel by train, compartments were fitted out luxuriously.

The engine-driver, fireman and guard on the old trains were brave men who were often called upon to perform heroic deeds. Today their task is considered as less dangerous but they are still responsible for the lives of many people, and have proved themselves worthy of the task.

A Russian locomotive, built in France. It can travel at 160km/h and is ideal for long journeys.

The train has become a comfortable and convenient mode of transport. The change from steam to diesel and electric power played an important part in the evolution of the railways.

THE BICYCLE

People have used wheels for 5,000 years, but it was not until 1790 that someone had the idea of mounting two in line in a frame and sitting between them. A Frenchman, Count Mède de Sivrac, rode astride what he called a *célérifère*, and propelled it along by pushing with his feet on the ground. His machine had drawbacks – it had no steering. But a similar machine built by Karl von Drais in 1817, the *Draisienne*, could be steered.

The bicycle, as a machine with pedals, was invented by Kirkpatrick Macmillan of Dumfriesshire in 1839. At last it was possible to get about under one's own steam at a speed which was faster than walking. In 1861, a man called Brunel, a French hat-maker, took his *Draisienne* to the workshop of the carriage manufacturer Michaux. Michaux's son thought the machine would be better if pedal-cranks were fixed to the front wheel so that it was possible to pedal along. Michaux didn't know about Macmillan's invention. And so the bicycle boom began. The pedal cycle took the public by storm. Track events made cycling even more popular. The first bicycle race took place in 1868 and was run in the Parc Saint-Cloud, in Paris, over a distance of 1,200m. The most famous race is the Tour de France, started in 1893 by the sporting journalist Henri Desgrange. Other important races take place in Italy, Spain and Switzerland.

A Michaux velocipede

A penny-farthing of 1875

A military bicycle

The French Count Mède de Sivrac on his strange machine called a *célérifère*. It had no pedals and had to be propelled along by the bicyclist, pushing with his feet on either side.

A bicycle built in 1880. This was still early days, and the designers attached most importance to the front wheel. The saddle and pedals were none too safe.

A curious race, held in 1888, on the Tours-Montlouis road in France, between men on horseback, cyclists and hounds. The course was 6km. At first the hounds were in the lead, but they were passed by the bicyclists. The horsemen were a long way behind. It was a triumph for the bicycle.

John Boyd Dunlop (1840–1921), the British inventor who developed the pneumatic tyre which bears his name.

The motorcycle followed the bicycle. It began with fixing a motor to a two-wheeled bicycle. The first model was built in 1869 by an unknown inventor who fixed a steam-powered motor to the Michaux bicycle frame. In the beginning the idea wasn't very successful, but it gradually gained ground because it was so useful and meant that the rider didn't have to get along by pedal-power. The motorcycle below is a strange early model with a rotary engine. Later, new models appeared on the market, leading to today's streamlined motorbikes.

Like many other inventions, the motorcycle has been adapted for use in war (van and rearguard, and offensive patrols).

THE MOTOR CAR

A horse-drawn carriage

The desire to make a vehicle driven by mechanical power goes back a very long way, but it came to a head in the mid-fifteenth century. It was at this time that the first drawings were made of vehicles which would use windpower by means of ingenious mechanisms. Another self-propelling vehicle appears in a drawing by Leonardo da Vinci.

The experiments of Papin and Watt with the steam engine were a great help when it came to making the first motor cars, because at first self-propelling vehicles used the only form of power then known, which was steam. The first experiment was made by the French military engineer Cugnot, who in 1771 built the three-wheeled truck or vehicle which is now in the Museum of Arts and Crafts in Paris. In 1883 Delamare-Deboutteville succeeded in making the first car driven by an internal combustion

benzine engine. Other early motor car designers were Daimler, Peugeot, Renault and Lenoir.

1885 was the most important year in the history of the motor car. It was then that the first cars with petrol engines were finally built, by two German mechanics, Benz and Daimler. They were associated later, and built cars under the name Mercedes-Benz.

Did you know . . .

. . . that there is another kind of internal combustion engine, which is mainly used in freight vehicles, on the railways and in ships? It is called the Diesel engine, after the name of its inventor, who was born in Paris, although his family originally came from Bavaria.

A 1907 Fiat racing car

An early Daimler model

The Cugnot truck

One-cylinder internal combustion engine (Barsanti and Matteuci, 1856).

Among the great motor races of the beginning of the twentieth century was the Vanderbilt Cup. The race was held for the last time in 1910. The picture shows the last winner arriving at the finish.

A Model T Ford of 1916, the first in the series. Fifteen million were sold in the United States in 19 years. It had a four-cylinder engine, metal bodywork throughout and could do 65km an hour. Ford was the first manufacturer to build cars on a production line.

As with most inventions, the car can be used in different ways in the fields of war, industry and agiculture. The tank and the Jeep were developed for military use, the lorry for carrying goods and the tractor for working in the fields.

This highly specialized car was built in Britain in 1929 and was called the Golden Arrow. If you look at the way it is designed, you will see why it was called that. It was the most powerful car of its day. Driven by Sir Henry Segrave, it beat the speed record of that time: 370km/h. The present record is 927km/h. As with other means of transport, man has tried to go faster and faster, breaking his own records.

The car, the invention which was dreamt of for so long, can be used in our time in endless ways – for rally driving, relaxation, excursions and holidays.

THE GRAMOPHONE

The idea of recording the human voice on an instrument which would be able to reproduce it faithfully was always one of man's dreams. In 1654 Cyrano de Bergerac wrote of pages which would reproduce the sound of music when rubbed by a needle. A Frenchman called Scott did some experiments by joining a very fine stylet or needle to a diaphragm with wax. In 1859 he was able to record the vibrations of the voice and musical sounds on treated paper, rolled round a rotating cylinder which he turned with a handle.

We owe the first phonograph or early gramophone to an American, Thomas Edison. His device, built in 1878, was capable of replaying a recording. It was made of a turning cylinder covered with a sheet of tin on which a needle was pressed, transmitting the vibrations picked up by a diaphragm and trumpet. The machine reproduced the original sound when played back, although it was rather distorted. Edison's invention took off when he experimented with recording telegraphic signals on a paper disc. The early gramophone above is in the Museum of Arts and Crafts in Paris.

Did you know . . .

. . . that according to the legend, King Midas's barber, unable to keep his master's secret (that the king had donkey's ears) any longer, told it to the earth after digging a hole which he then hurriedly filled in again? But some rushes grew on the very same spot, and every time the wind blew, they repeated to the passers-by: 'Midas, King Midas has ass's ears!' If we are to believe the legend, this was the first recording of the human voice.

. . . that the name phonograph is derived from the word 'phonoautograph' which means 'voice which records itself'?

. . . that among the men who did experiments before Edison were Young, who had the idea of joining a needle to a vibrating object and registering the vibrations on a turning cylinder; Duhamel, who recorded the vibrations of strings; and Wertheim, who did experiments joining a needle to tuning forks?

Shown below is Edison's second phonograph, made in 1889. It caused great amazement, disbelief and admiration. To have a record of the human voice seemed miraculous. The gramophone had a great influence on people's tastes and habits.

Before the gramophone, one way of playing recorded music was the barrel organ or piano organ which was played by turning a handle. It could be wheeled along, and was often played in the street.

The famous actress, Sarah Bernhardt, recording her voice in a New York studio. The phonograph opened up endless possibilities.

A great stride forward was made by the German Berliner, who in the 1880s replaced the cylinder with a horizontal disc. On the right is a gramophone of the 1920s.

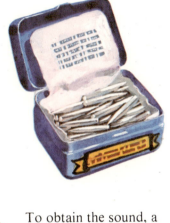

To obtain the sound, a needle was used which followed the vibrations recorded in the groove and reproduced the sound with varying degrees of success.

As with most inventions that have had a profound effect on our way of life, it took a long time to develop the gramophone from its primitive form to the highly technical and sophisticated instrument it is today.

Record-players, cassettes, microphones and tape-recorders are part of the world of recorded sound which is part of our civilization. Both classical and modern music can be perfectly reproduced. Everything can be 'canned'.

THE CINEMA

Before the days of the cinema, a little man, rather like a medieval street musician, wandered through the streets with a strange box which everyone called a 'magic lantern'. This apparatus had been designed in 1645 by the Austrian professor Athanasius Kircher, and for many years it caused terror and amusement to everyone who saw it. We know now that the secret of the magic lantern was a lamp, the light from which was reflected by a mirror through a glass slide, projecting an enlarged image of what was painted on the glass on to a screen. Later, the pictures were replaced by photographs. The cinema, which employed a succession of images to give the impression of movement, was not long in following.

Magic lantern

Did you know . . .

. . . that a certain Doctor Roget invented the magic disc in 1825? On one side was a picture of a cage, and on the other, a picture of a parrot. When the disc was turned fast enough on its string, it looked as though the bird was sitting in the cage.

. . . that when one of the first documentaries, called *A train arriving at the station*, was shown, the public were afraid of being squashed by the engine?

The cage

The parrot

The parrot in the cage

The zöetrope created an illusion of movement by means of a rotating disc on which figures were painted. Each figure was seen momentarily through a slot as the disc spun round.

In 1895, Edison did some experiments with the kinetoscope, a kind of peepshow. The Lumière brothers of France improved on this invention by designing the first apparatus for projecting photographs, called the 'cinematograph'.

The device of the two Frenchmen, the Lumière brothers, projected the pictures from a strip of photographic film on to the screen.

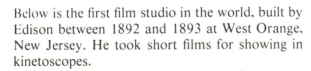

Below is the first film studio in the world, built by Edison between 1892 and 1893 at West Orange, New Jersey. He took short films for showing in kinetoscopes.

The cinema owed its first real success to the inventive genius of the Frenchman Georges Méliès, who with his story films and printed captions gave the medium a new dimension. He is shown here dressed and made up to play in a film.

In 1877, Eadweard Muybridge took a great series of photographs using up to 24 cameras arranged to catch the different movements of a horse and rider. By joining these photographs, different successive positions could give the appearance of continuous movement. This is the principle of cine film, but it was not until 20 years later that the cinema was invented.

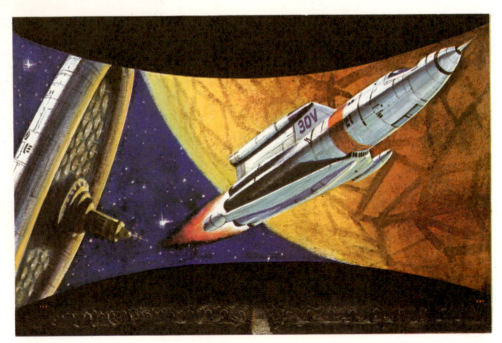

The use of enormously wide screens gives the modern cinemagoer the impression that he is taking part in the scene. The cinema has come a long way; from silent to talking films, from black-and-white to colour, and from a fairground show to an artistic production.

PHOTOGRAPHY

The first lens used in a 'camera obscura' bu Cardano in 1550 was based on observations made by Leonardo da Vinci 50 years before. This early lens of Cardano's was about the size of a car headlamp. It was used for projecting images on a whitened wall in a dark room. The next step in the development of the camera was to reduce the room in size to a box, which was achieved thanks to the work of Cesare Cesariano, a monk called Pafnuzio and the scientist Mamolico. In 1589 the Italian scientist Jean-Baptiste della Porta was acclaimed as the inventor of the camera obscura. It was a perfect model, almost identical in the way it worked to today's fixed focus, plate or box cameras. Then a sensational discovery was made in 1826 when Niépce succeeded in printing the first real photograph. Three years later Niépce and Daguerre became friends, and their friendship did much to further the progress of photography. Fox Talbot, Le Gray, Scott Archer, Dixon, Maddox, Goodwin and others made further improvements to the camera, leading on to the advanced photographic equipment of today.

The first Kodak Box Brownie

The Vest Pocket Kodak

Early photographic equipment

An early Leica

Jean-Baptiste della Porta noticed that if light rays passed through a hole in a wall, the images of the objects outside the wall appeared upside down on the wall opposite. It was in this way that he discovered his camera obscura.

Niépce and Daguerre were pioneers of photography. Their collaboration gave an enormous boost to the new invention. Daguerre discovered a method of reproducing images which was called the 'daguerreotype' process. In the lower picture you can see one of the first daguerreotypes: note the fine quality and artistic subject matter, obtained with an exposure of six minutes.

A folding camera with which you can take good photographs. Here are also shown some of the equipment used in developing, printing and enlarging. The negative produced by the camera is turned into a positive print, showing the original image. Photography plays an important role in medicine, metallurgy and astronomy. It can be both highly technical and artistic.

A Polaroid camera, invented by E. S. Land and first marketed in 1948. It has the advantage of giving a positive print in a few seconds.

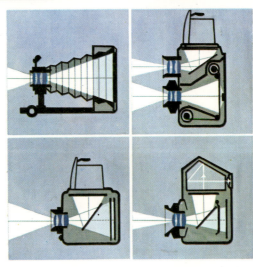

Four types of camera of different construction. Notice the position of the lens and of the focal plane.

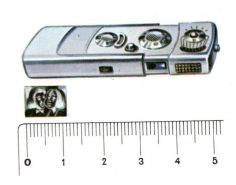

A sub-miniature camera, which takes negatives measuring 8mm by 11mm. It has no diaphragm; the light meter is coupled with the shutter speeds. Used by spies and secret agents since World War II, it can easily be carried in a small pocket.

THE TELEPHONE

With the invention of the telephone, it became possible to transmit the human voice over a distance. Now that this invention is part of our daily life it is almost impossible to realize what the discovery meant when it was first made; it allowed people for the first time to feel close to those who were far away by speaking to them.

There are arguments as to who was the original inventor of the telephone. Everything seems to indicate that the pioneer in the field was Antonio Meucci, an Italian living in the United States who thought up a system for making short-distance calls. In 1871 he was living in Clifton, near New York, and he applied for a patent for his device, which was made from a thin metal plate connected to an electro-magnet. Five years later, in America, two other men applied for a patent, with only two hours between their applications, for a fairly similar type of instrument. They were a Scottish scientist, Alexander Graham Bell, and an electrician called Elisha Gray. So three men were disputing the patent, and later ten others joined in, including Edison. This led to a complex trial, until in 1886 the Supreme Court of the United States pronounced in favour of Graham Bell. The illustration shows a Siemens telephone, the first manufactured model on the market.

Did you know . . .

. . . that Professor Graham Bell succeeded in inventing his telephone while he was devoting his life to helping the deaf and dumb in Boston, USA?

. . . that the telephone's first triumph was when Bell said to the friend who was helping him: 'Mr Watson, come here; I want you'? With these words, transmitted from one room to another, the telephone era had begun.

. . . that setting up the telephone took a long time and the first 'long-distance' call of 22km wasn't made until 1877?

. . . that one of the first people to have a telephone installed was Queen Victoria?

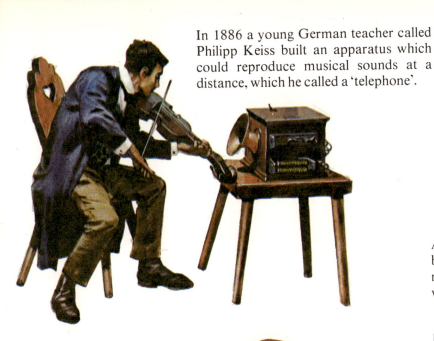

In 1886 a young German teacher called Philipp Keiss built an apparatus which could reproduce musical sounds at a distance, which he called a 'telephone'.

Above is the first telephone Graham Bell built, which was better than those of Meucci and Gray. It was very rudimentary, as you can see, but it enabled the first telephone conversation to be made, in 1876.

By the 1880s the first telephone exchanges were operating in the United States.

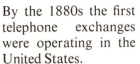

At the top is the earpiece, housing a diaphragm and an electromagnet. Below is the mouthpiece with diaphragm and carbon granules.

Cable ships are used in setting up overseas telecommunications. They lay lines by means of underwater cables.

As long-distance calls grew in popularity, people began to make different types of telephone, for example these early wall and table telephones, and today there are many elegant and practical models.

The telephone is so useful that it is not surprising it is used all over the world. Today, for example, it is very easy to speak to New York from Paris. Like the aeroplane, the telephone has made the world smaller.

EDISON'S ELECTRIC LIGHT BULB

Sunlight, moonlight and the light from fires enabled our ancestors of long ago to avoid being in total darkness. Gradually, torches, wax candles, oil and paraffin lamps, and finally gas lights banished the shadows and allowed people, to some extent, to carry on their work or play at night. Gas lighting was a great advance, but it was not until the nineteenth century that the first electric light became a reality. In 1813, Humphry Davy did an experiment with the electric arc in the basement of the Royal Institution in London, using a large battery producing 2,000 volts. The first electric lamp was Davy's egg, which worked on the principle of the arc lamp. Lighting with arc lamps powered by a dynamo appeared in various European capitals at the end of the nineteenth century. The Mansion House in London was lit by Siemens lights. But arc lights were too bright and had to be dimmed by shades; many people thought the old gas lights were better. Then came the first electric filament bulb, an invention which was the work of Thomas Alva Edison in the United States and Joseph Swan in England.

Did you know ...

... that Edison, besides inventing the electric light bulb, patented over a thousand inventions and is therefore considered a great benefactor of humanity?

... that the bulb in the illustration on the right is one of four kinds invented by Edison? He used carbon, which doesn't melt, and carbonized bamboo.

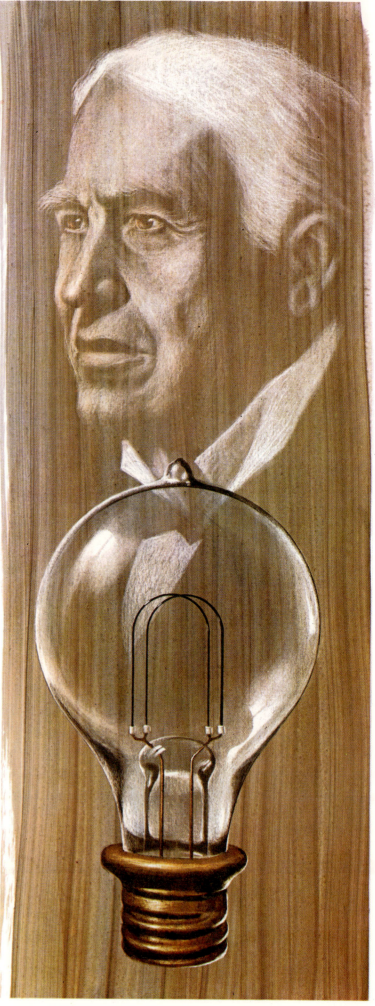

Flaming torch

Wax candle in a candleholder

Gaslight

For a long time, writers and philosophers, or anyone who wanted to read by night, had to use oil or paraffin lamps, which often caused eyestrain or permanent eye damage.

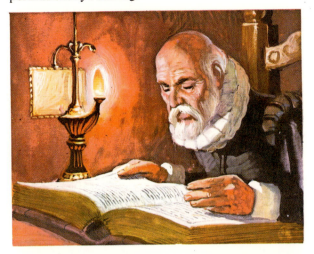

On the left, Davy's electric egg. An arc light based on this invention was placed on the engine of the Moscow–Koursk train, in which the Tsar travelled.

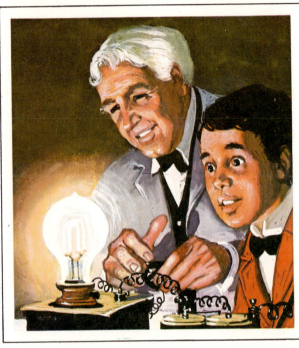

Alva Edison worked tirelessly to find the right filament for his bulb. With his assistant, he tried out 2,000 different kinds of filament.

New York had electric lighting before the end of the nineteenth century. The early Osmium and tantalum filaments were later replaced by tungsten.

From the time when Edison used a strip of carbonized bamboo, which he had taken from the fan of one of his admirers, until the present day, a series of technical innovations have helped to perfect electric lighting.

Astronauts orbiting Earth can tell where different cities are from the brightness of their lights.

We mustn't let the way we can so easily and conveniently switch on an electric light today allow us to forget the long process of invention which gave us the electric light bulb.

RADIO

When man first evolved, radio waves already existed in his natural surroundings. The vibrations are produced by a spark jumping between two clouds or between a cloud and the earth, or by other atmospheric phenomena. As early as 1795 there were men who thought that in the not too distant future people would be able to communicate with each other from a distance. The work of a long line of scientists, such as Faraday, Maxwell, Federson, Hughes and Hertz, enabled an Italian, Guglielmo Marconi, to send the first wireless message in 1897.

The scene was set for the major invention of the radio, and Marconi made use of Branly's coherer and Popoff's aerial. Later, from 1902 to 1906, further improvements were made by Fleming with his diode and Lee De Forest with the grid. Radios began to be used in the field of industry, and wirelesses receiving and transmitting messages were invaluable on ships. In 1909 the *Republic* was saved thanks to one of these Morse transmitting sets and in 1912 a few of the *Titanic*'s passengers were able to be saved because of the transmitted SOS call.

Guglielmo Marconi gave a great boost to telecommunications when he invented a set in which the transmitter and receiver were not joined by wires. One of these sets is shown below.

Theory became practice when radio sets activated by crystals and equipped with headphones allowed the listener to hear music and the presenter's voice.

Old radio sets contained wires and valves, like the one shown on the left. Valves have now been replaced by transistors, the minute size of which is a great advantage in electronic layouts. Modern radios only need small batteries, which means that portable sets can be made, not much bigger than a packet of cigarettes.

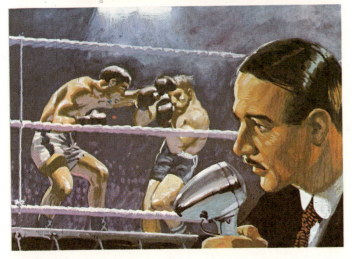

The great age of radio began when radio broadcasts of sporting, cultural and political events were introduced. In 1921 the world heavyweight boxing championship between Dempsey and Carpentier was broadcast. The public bought sets by the thousand. The commentator's voice described the match, blow by blow. The radio, as a means of mass communication, was born, and its influence would go on growing.

In modern radio sets the mass of wires which made up the circuit has been replaced by the 'printed' circuit. The illustration above shows a modern radio set, with the circuit shown behind it. The efficiency and practical size of these modern sets have contributed to their popularity today.

TELEVISION

Camera with monitor incorporated

The invention of television followed on from the discovery of radio telegraphy. To begin with, however, television transmission depended on wires. The German Alfred Korn was the first to experiment in this way. Then John Baird made his successful experiments. Later, Nipkow made notable advances, including the use of a pierced metal disk. Vladimir

Zworykin introduced the electronic tube. Later, various other scientists contributed to the development of television, including Belin, Barthélémy, Von Ardenne and Fischer. Regular transmissions to the public began in 1932, in London. The 1939 war put a halt to television services. The radio was then at its most popular and no one dreamt that the new invention could replace it. After 1945 new research meant that television came into its own.

When sets became available to a mass market, the success of television surpassed all expectations. In time, further technical improvements were made, and high-quality programmes of great interest could be shown. A memorable example was the historic landing on the Moon – a great moment for all mankind – which was brought to us direct on our television screens.

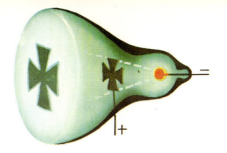

We owe the practical application of Paul Nipkow's disc to television transmissions to the British scientist John Logie Baird. The first official television broadcasts in 1929 used Baird's system. The illustration on the left shows the receiver with which Baird obtained his pictures. He died almost forgotten in 1946.

The cathode ray tube receives information in the form of electrical signals. This information is converted into pictures by bombarding a specially-treated screen with electrons.

Television tube. The electron gun is in the neck of the glass covering of the tube.

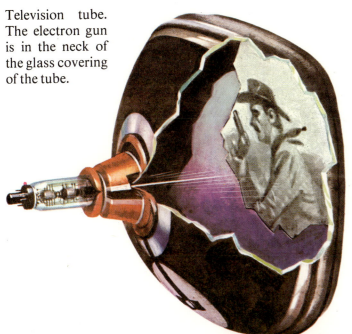

Picking up the televised picture and transmission. The scene to be transmitted is filmed in the studio you can see in the background. In the foreground is the audio visual recording room. Specialist technicians control the scanning of the picture.

The glass screen of the television tube must be thick. If it was thin it would break because of the low pressure inside. Since the advent of plastics, screens have been given an outer layer which won't shatter, and, if the worst comes to the worst, will only crack. These protective casings are in polyester resin reinforced with fibreglass, shaped to the tube and fastened with special adhesives.

Television plays an important role in industry in controlling phases of production, and other important uses are in closed-circuit television and in cultural and scientific activities. It is an invention which still has great untapped possibilities. It was thanks to television that radar, which plays such a vital role in navigation, was invented.

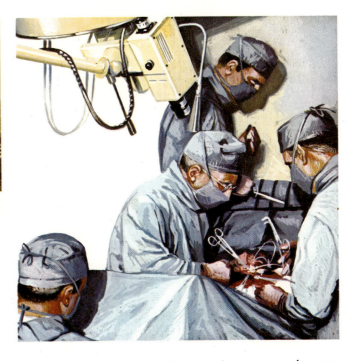

It is possible today for medical students to watch a surgical operation on closed-circuit television, or for us to view it on our own television screens.

STEEL

Steel is a mixture of iron, carbon and other ingredients, fused in a furnace. Man knew about iron in 1000 BC, but its use was limited by its brittleness. Steel, which is much less brittle, is made from iron by removing excess carbon. Once the process for making it was mastered, steel proved to be one of man's most useful inventions. It was used for making agricultural implements and high-quality weapons such as the swords made in Toledo and Damascus.

For many years, craftsmen made steel in small quantities in crucibles. Smelting in large furnaces was only introduced in the 1850s. The Bessemer process, patented by Henry Bessemer in 1856, employs a blast of cold air to remove excess carbon and convert the iron into steel. The Martin-Siemens open-hearth process, perfected by Karl Wilhelm Siemens in 1866, uses blasts of preheated air and combustible gas. It produces very high quality steel. In 1898 the age of electro-metallurgy began with the construction of electric furnaces for making special steels. The steel, once made, is cast into ingots or poured in the liquid state into a casting ladle for use in special moulds. As you can see from the picture below, the heat and glare from the liquid metal are blindingly intense.

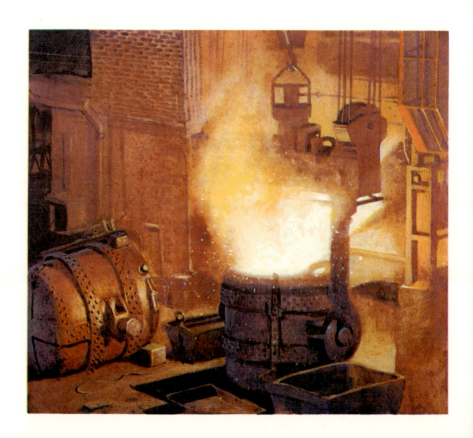

Iron tools of 1000 BC; top to bottom: dagger, ploughshare, arrowheads and a sickle.

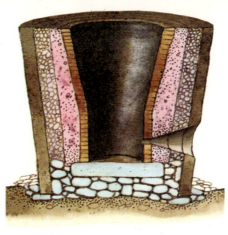

An early blast furnace for smelting iron, known as the Osmund furnace. It dates from the Middle Ages.

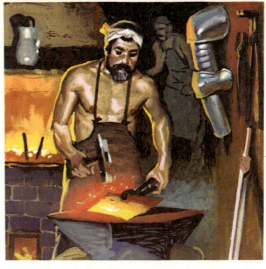

An ancient forge. The iron was heated until it was red hot, softening it and enabling the smith to beat it into the required shape.

The Bessemer steel-making process. An egg-shaped converter is used.

The tempering of steel. When heated from 20°C to 1,000°C its structure changes; allowed to cool naturally, it reverts to its original structure, but any elements which make it brittle are dispersed.

If the steel is cooled rapidly, the structure it has at 1,000°C can be retained when the metal is cold. This process is used to harden steel.

Products made from steel

Developed from the early furnaces, such as the Catalan hearth or forge, the Osmund furnace and the open puddling furnace, today's modern furnaces are built to produce steel in great quantities.

One of the stages in the steel-making process is rolling. Modern automated machinery is used in today's plants and top right are some pieces of steel which have been rolled. The steel is teemed into ingot-moulds and the ingots pass through a series of rolling-mills to obtain the finished products. Steel production is one of the things which indicate the industrial and economic strength of a country.

THE AEROPLANE

One of man's oldest dreams has been to be able to fly like a bird. But his first successful attempts were not in an aeroplane, but in lighter than air craft such as the Montgolfier brothers' balloon and the dirigible – inventions which for a good many years made people forget their experiments with the flight of vehicles heavier than air. But the drawbacks of these earlier craft finally led to the belief that the aeroplane was the machine most suitable for taking off from the ground and flying through the air. Experience proved that those who thought so were indeed correct. Clément Ader's *Eole* was the first flying-machine to take off successfully. On 17 December 1903 the Wright brothers succeeded in making the world's first flight in a self-propelled aircraft.

A Curtiss aeroplane of the 1930s

The illustration on the left shows a project of Leonardo da Vinci; he was working on a helicopter and various systems of beating wings, worked by springs and based on the muscle structure of birds. On the right is a hang-glider built by Lilienthal, who was killed during one of his flights.

An aeroplane built by the Frenchman Ader in 1897. He had studied the flight of storks and bats in detail while working on his invention, and the machine is in fact like an enormous bird with folding wings. Although his attempt at flight was a total failure, his machine can still be seen today in Paris.

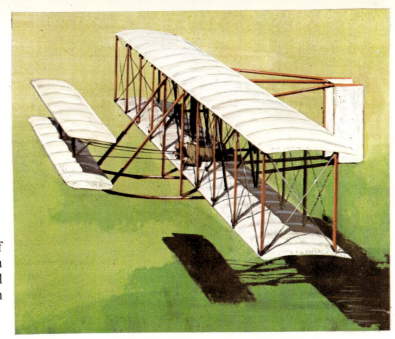

Man's fascination with flight is illustrated by the myth of Icarus, who tried to reach the sun with wings attached with wax. On the right is the Wright brothers' first successful motor-propelled aircraft. The aeroplane, built in the USA in 1903, stayed in the air for about 59 seconds.

In 1909 Blériot crossed the Channel; in 1927 Charles Lindbergh flew from New York to Paris non-stop in his *Spirit of St Louis*, a specially-built Ryan monoplane.

During World War I the aeroplane played a secondary role; it was different in World War II. Shown above are some of the aeroplanes which took part in the Battle of Britain. Left, top to bottom: Boulton-Paul Defiant, Spitfire and Messerschmitt 109; right, top to bottom: JU-87 (Stuka), DO-17 and Messerschmitt 110.

The aeroplanes of World War II are already museum pieces. New types of aircraft appeared in the postwar years. Today supersonic aircraft attain speeds which were never dreamt of in the past. At the top of the picture are Phantoms from America; below, the Anglo-French Concorde.

The development of the aeroplane has not stopped at supersonic aircraft. In the very near future the conventional rocket will be replaced by space vehicles which, having re-entered the Earth's atmosphere, will be able to land at an airfield and be refitted for future missions.

REINFORCED CONCRETE

While the use of iron in architecture was being developed, another type of construction, based on iron combined with cement, was introduced. Even in the distant past, in Roman times, it was known that a mixture of quicklime and clay or pozzolana mixed with water would set to become very hard. But this material was not used with reinforcement until 1774, the year when John Smeaton used a mixture of mortar and pieces of iron in masonry. In 1868 the gardener Monnier used iron bars when making a concrete pond. The combination of iron and concrete made what is known as 'reinforced concrete', or more precisely, 'reinforced cement'. Iron alone was not resistant enough, and cement alone would not bear all the stress it would necessarily be subjected to when used as a supporting structure.

Reinforced concrete has given rise to some very original architectural creations, because it has very different characteristics from those of iron. In 1890 the French architect Hennebique built his own house in the new material: hanging gardens, a spiral staircase and decorative elements on the upper part of the façade demonstrated the possibilities opened up by reinforced concrete. Later, other original projects were undertaken.

But reinforced cement didn't only prove useful in architecture; it could also be used in engineering projects, such as the building of large dams. Above is shown the Kariba dam, which was completed in 1966. It is in Rhodesia, on the Zambezi, and is the largest dam in Africa. The water from the open sluices makes a deafening roar.

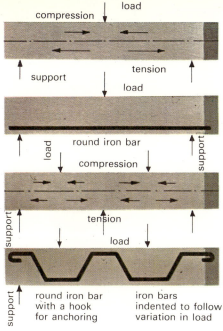

Reinforced concrete is a conglomerate of cement, sand and gravel mixed with water, and reinforced with iron internally. it resists bending and stretching. In sections two and four of the diagram, iron bars with a circular section and with hooks or indentations to follow the variations in load have been introduced. In sections one and three there is no iron, and the concrete is likely to break. The arrows above each section indicate the load to be carried, and those below indicate the supports.

In 1774 John Smeaton built the Eddystone Lighthouse, the first example of successful concrete construction.

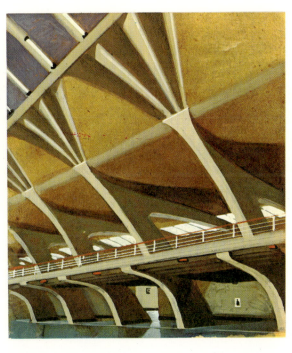

Bridge over the Arve (Geneva, 1937), built by the Swiss Robert Maillard. Everything that isn't functional has been eliminated. The picture on the right shows how a modern technique (ferro-concrete) has been used by the Italian Nervi for the construction of the roof of the Exhibition Hall in Turin.

A skyscraper apartment building in Marina City, USA, called the Round Towers. You can see all over Chicago from the top.

The famous bridge of Oosterschelde, in Holland, the longest bridge in Europe. This striking construction in reinforced concrete, with a series of very solid supports, is part of an unending struggle with the sea. The danger of being inundated has been threatening the Dutch for 1,200 years, and the country is protected by dykes and dunes which stretch for a total length of 1,800km.

METAL CONSTRUCTION

Before the industrial age, iron was used very sparingly and only as an addition to buildings, not as an integral part of them. There were two reasons for this; its rarity and the way it was affected by atmospheric conditions. At the end of the eighteenth century people started talking about producing iron on an industrial scale. The first iron rails for railways were made in 1767 and a few years later the world's first iron bridge was built. This showed that parts of a building could be made in advance and put together on the site. It was an alliance between industry and architecture.

The production of iron on an industrial scale meant that metal buildings of great beauty and originality could be built. One of these striking buildings, a triumph of French engineering, is of course the Eiffel Tower in Paris. Built by the engineer Gustave Eiffel for the Universal Exhibition in Paris in 1889, it represented an enormous advance in the development of the new technique of metal construction.

The American James Bogardus was the first to build commercial buildings with a metal framework. He built shops and offices. The outer walls of many of these buildings were reduced to an almost continuous surface of iron and glass, although columns sometimes added a Renaissance touch and iron arches were used between the columns.

Between 1775 and 1779 a sensational event occurred in the history of metal architecture: Abraham Darby built the first iron bridge, over the Severn in England. The bridge had a single arch and was made in two sections.

A metal framework is used to provide the structural strength of modern building, allowing greater architectural flexibility. Bogardus was the pioneer in these experiments and built metal-frame houses of great solidity. He proved that even if the greater part of the building was destroyed, the metal frame remained standing.

One of the first suspension bridges with metal cables was built by Marc Seguin in 1824. He imitated bridges in America where hemp cables or strips of leather had been used. The Forth railway bridge in Scotland, shown above, was built between 1882 and 1890. It uses the cantilever principle, in which the main spans are balanced on central piers and connected by secondary spans.

While markets with a thin metal framework such as those of the Madeleine and Les Halles were being built in France, in America they were concentrating on building skyscrapers. The first of these, shown above, was built in 1885. The work of William Le Baron Jenney, it became the Home Insurance Co. of Chicago. It had ten storeys and was built with a metal framework, according to modern construction techniques. Other skyscrapers followed, particularly in New York, where they were fantastically high.

The most famous suspension bridge in the world is the Golden Gate Bridge in San Francisco, California. It was built to avoid the long detour which previously had to be made round the coast. It was opened in 1937 and is a magnificent structure in a magnificent setting.

THE ROBOT

We all know what a robot is because we have seen one at the cinema or on television, and many of us have read science-fiction stories about mechanical men or androids. However, many people probably do not know that these ingenious mechanisms were being made centuries ago. The legendary architect Daedalus, who built the Cretan Labyrinth with its Minotaur, is said to have made statues which could move and walk, and there is a story that Archytas of Tarentum made a pigeon which flew. These are only legends, but the legends lived on till the Middle Ages and alchemists believed they were true, because they were obsessed with the idea of making an artificial man. They did not realize that it was a purely technical problem to make an automaton. A robot is simply an automatic mechanism which can do the things humans do and which acts as if it had human intelligence.

It was in about 1700 that the golden age of automatons or mechanical dolls began. The most famous was Baron Von Kempelen's 'Turk' (shown below), a chess-playing android which sat with its legs inside a chest, on which was a chess-board. It was operated by a complicated system of levers, gears, springs and pistons inside the chest.

A science-fiction robot

Did you know . . .

. . . that the first automaton worthy of being recorded was the cock on Strasbourg Cathedral, made in 1354, which appeared on the hour, beat its wings and crowed three times?

. . . that in 1738 there was an exhibition of automatons in Paris, and there was one which could play the flute and was capable of playing twelve different tunes?

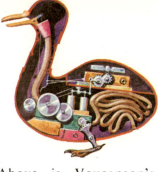

Above is Vaucanson's duck. It moved, swam, beat its wings and performed other natural functions. The automaton on the left is Droz's artist. When operated, it drew very accurate pictures.

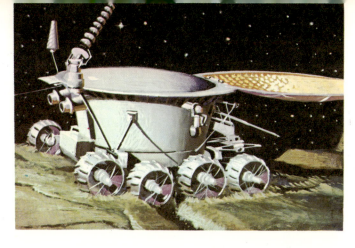

Lunokhod 1 was the first robot spacecraft to land on the Moon. It was the work of Russian scientists. An authentic thinking robot, it can pick up rocks, analyse them and transmit the results back to Earth.

A Chinese Suan-Pan abacus or counting-frame, built for mechanical calculations long ago. It was made of bamboo rods on which were threaded little ivory balls.

A calculating machine appeared in 1885 – the Macaroni Box. The keys were little rods; the guide-keys were metal pins.

Pascal's arithmetic machine of 1642. The wheels were divided from zero to nine, and when one of them rotated ten places, it rotated the one on the left one place.

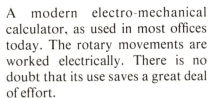

A modern electro-mechanical calculator, as used in most offices today. The rotary movements are worked electrically. There is no doubt that its use saves a great deal of effort.

On the right you can see a group of computers worked by specialist technicians who monitor every movement. One of them is printing on a keyboard the information to feed into the system; another works the control panel; and the third is checking the information given. The information furnished is represented by perforations in a tape and is 'read' by a photoelectric cell. The data is collected together in the 'memory', which is made of silicon chip integrated circuits.

We have gone on from mechanical calculators to electronic computers. Men feed the information to the machine and it does the rest. The mechanized robot has become an electronic brain which can think and act on programmed information.

THE ATOM BOMB

After the atom-splitting experiments made by Einstein, Bohr, Rutherford, Fermi and other scientists, people were shocked to realize that man now had the most deadly weapon he had possessed in his entire history: the atom bomb. To make it, uranium-235 and plutonium were used. In 1939, fearing that Nazi Germany would make a nuclear weapon, a group of scientists asked the American president, Roosevelt, to forestall Germany by making an atom bomb. So Project Manhattan was started in the United States, involving some of the best physicists in the world. The first atom bomb was tried out in June 1945 in the New Mexico desert. In August the same year, two bombs were dropped on Japan – one on Hiroshima and the other on Nagasaki; they caused terrible destruction. A Boeing B-29 called *Enola Gay* was used to carry the bomb.

Type of bomb used at Hiroshima

Height of a man compared with the bomb

Type of bomb used at Nagasaki

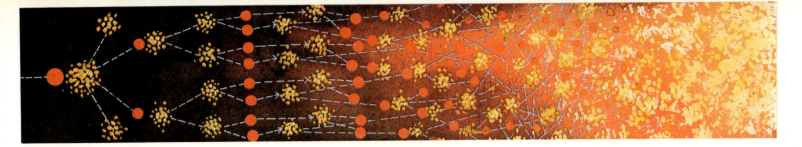

A nuclear chain reaction: it liberates an enormous amount of energy. The uranium nucleus, hitting a neutron, splits into two fragments and shoots out two neutrons. If one of them bombards another uranium nucleus the process is repeated and more energy is liberated. If both neutrons each bombard a nucleus, the process is multiplied.

In 1933, Albert Einstein left Germany to escape from Nazi persecution and went to the United States. He was one of the brains behind the atom bomb.

Le Roy Lehman, the American pilot, dropped the bomb on Japan without knowing it was a nuclear weapon. He was horrified, and retired to a monastery.

Affected chromosomes and genes

Normal chromosomes and genes. Passed on from generation to generation, they give us our hereditary characteristics.

Chromosomes affected by atomic radiation. The arrowed chromosomes are broken and will not retain their structure.

This is how they will reshape. These chromosomes will lead to abnormal babies being born, because of the effects of radioactivity.

One of the most important postwar developments in the field of naval propulsion is the atomic submarine. Nuclear energy, which was first used as a destructive force, is now being used as a force for progress. In this category is the atomic submarine *Nautilus*, built in the United States in 1955, which was the first to make the voyage under the polar ice-cap without stopping to refuel. The illustration shows the Soviet ice-breaker *Lenin*, the first atomic ship for ocean navigation; it can go for two years without needing to take on more fuel.

A simple nuclear reactor is submerged in a reservoir of water. This serves to control the nuclear reaction. The radiation causes a brilliant glow.

THE ROCKET

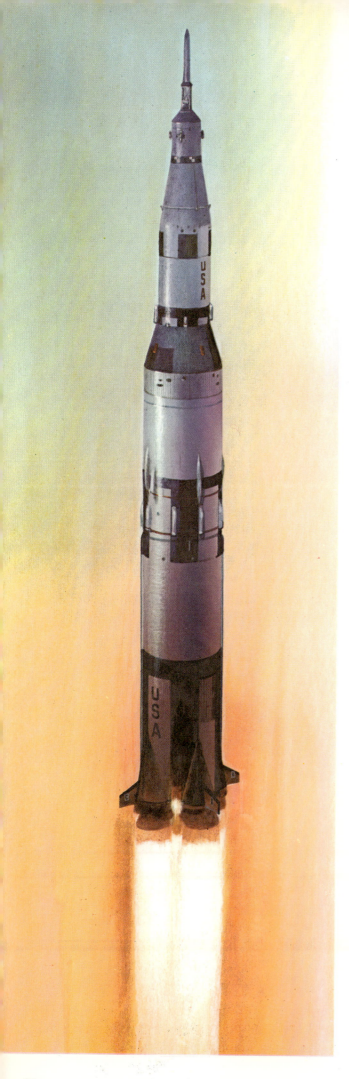

The desire to conquer space is as old as man's longing to fly. The legend of Icarus, who tried to fly to the sun, reflects man's wish to travel beyond this planet. In the mid-seventeenth century, the French author Cyrano de Bergerac published a work in which he anticipated rockets and the manned capsule of the American project Mercury. Other authors wrote about space voyages; for instance Samosata, Kepler, Edgar Allan Poe and Jules Verne. Then science took over from the imagination, and scientists replaced the novelists. Foremost among them were a Russian, Tsiolkovskii, and a German, Oberth, the pioneers and fathers of modern space flight. In Tsiolkovskii's day, inadequate and unstable balloons were being used as aircraft. The aeroplane was still a dream, but the Russian professor was already thinking of flights which would go beyond the Earth's atmosphere. He was convinced that only a rocket would be able to undertake such an ambitious project. In Germany, Oberth and Von Braun worked on space rockets such as the V2, the precursors of the rockets of today. The illustration on the left shows a rocket being launched. The violent expulsion of gas from the bottom of the rocket creates the force to propel it upwards.

In 1957 the Russians launched the first Sputnik into space, and the Americans put the Explorer and the Pioneer into orbit. The sky became full of artificial satellites carrying out exploratory missions, technical and scientific research, preliminary to the first manned space flight. This was carried out successfully in 1961 by the Soviet cosmonaut Yuri Gagarin. The rocket had become a reality, and man's ambition to land on the Moon was realized by the American project Apollo. In 1969, Armstrong, Aldrin and Collins, on board Apollo 11, landed on this satellite of the Earth.

Space flight has only just begun. Up till now, enormous booster rockets have been needed to launch man on his flight into space. Will it be possible in the future to invent a machine which will be able to take off under its own power to explore the universe? Man has reached the Moon, but there are plenty of other wonders in space waiting to be discovered.

Left, the artificial satellite Sputnik and far left, the V2.

An American space capsule, with pressurized cabin for the crew. It is the manned part of the projectile and can house three astronauts.

Yuri Gagarin, the first cosmonaut

Neil Armstrong, the US astronaut who, on board Apollo 11 in July 1969 was the first man to land on the Moon. Thanks to television, the whole world could witness the most daring feat in the history of mankind.

John C. Houbolt, the American engineer who was the inventor of the lunar module. He succeeded in getting his system for landing and taking off from the lunar surface adopted in spite of the contrary views of Von Braun and other very important members of NASA, the space flight organization.

The command module and the lunar module which had travelled together, separating. The lunar module lands gently on the Moon.

The astronaut has got out of the lunar module and walks on the surface of the Moon, protected by his special space-suit; an historic moment.

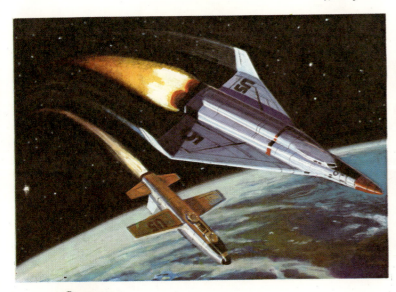

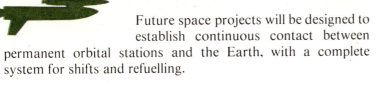

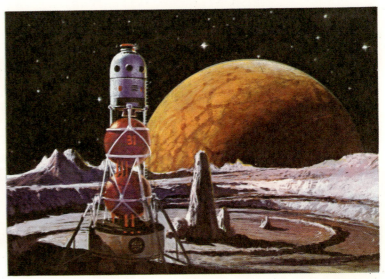

Future space projects will be designed to establish continuous contact between permanent orbital stations and the Earth, with a complete system for shifts and refuelling.

A science-fiction dream which will one day perhaps be a reality, showing a strangely shaped spacecraft about to take off. Beyond, the planet Mars; the craft is on a satellite of Mars, and will take off for Mars from there.